THE PIOUS CAT

KU-350-571

A HUNGRY CAT ONCE STOLE INTO A FARMER'S KITCHEN.

CURDS! HM-M-M...

?!

OH, DEAR! THE RIM OF THE POT IS STILL ROUND MY NECK!

I GUESS I'M STUCK WITH IT.

I SAY! I LOOK GOOD IN IT! A HOLY CHAIN FOR THE HOLY CAT!

AND NOW TO THE FOREST.

SHE DID NOT TRY TO CATCH ME! WHAT AN UNUSUAL CAT!

THE CURIOUS PEACOCK HOPPED AFTER THE CAT.

WHERE ARE YOU OFF TO?

BY THIS HOLY NECKLACE OF LORD KEDAR, I RENOUNCE THE WAY OF BEASTS OF PREY. IN THE HOLY RIVER, LET'S WASH OUR SINS AWAY. COME, FRIEND, TWO IS BETTER THAN ONE.

I'LL GO WITH YOU. TOGETHER WE'LL BATHE IN THE HOLY GANGA.

AS THE TWO WALKED ON —

HOW STRANGE! THEY JUST WALKED PAST WITHOUT SO MUCH AS A GLANCE AT ME!

HE FLEW AFTER THEM.

WHERE ARE YOU OFF TO?

TO THE HOLY GANGA. TO WASH OFF OUR PAST. FOR BY THIS NECKLACE OF LORD KEDAR I'VE VOWED TO GIVE UP SIN! COME WITH US, BROTHER, FOR THREE IS BETTER THAN TWO.

I'LL COME. OH, I'LL COME TOO! TOGETHER WE'LL BATHE IN THE HOLY GANGA.

A LITTLE FURTHER AWAY THEY MET A MOUSE. WHEN HE HEARD WHERE THEY WERE GOING —

I'VE ALWAYS WANTED TO GO ON A PILGRIMAGE. I'LL GO WITH YOU.

SO THE CAT, THE PEACOCK, THE PIGEON AND THE MOUSE JOURNEYED ON...

...TILL AT NIGHTFALL, THEY CAME UPON A HUT IN THE FOREST.

LET'S REST HERE TONIGHT. I WILL SPEAK TO YOU OF DHARMA AND KARMA. THEN WE SHALL SING HYMNS.

IT IS OUR DUTY TO PROTECT THE LIVING. TO KILL IS SINFUL...

THE CAT PREACHED ON. BUT HER MIND WAS ON OTHER THINGS.

SOON THE DEVOTEES STOOD UP. THE CAT HELD UP THE CYMBALS...

...AND BEGAN CLANGING THEM RHYTHMICALLY. THE DEVOTEES BEGAN TO DANCE.

FASTER AND FASTER WENT THE RHYTHM. THE DEVOTEES DANCED ON IN A FRENZY...

...WHILE THE CAT'S EYES WERE BLOOD-SHOT AS SHE DRIBBLED.

SUDDENLY, THE CAT JUMPED DOWN FROM THE PLATFORM...

... DANCED UP TO THE ENTRANCE...

...AND BLOCKED IT. THEN SHE DROPPED THE CYMBALS TO THE FLOOR.

CLANG

THE MOUSE WAS THE FIRST TO SENSE TROUBLE.

OH! OH! I'D BETTER DIG A HOLE FAST!

YOU VAIN PEACOCK! WHOM WOULD YOU WOO WITH THAT DISPLAY OF FEATHERS?

GOD GAVE ME THESE FEATHERS, HOLY ONE. I CANNOT BUT DISPLAY THEM. I...I...

WHILE THE CAT BAITED THE PEACOCK THE MOUSE FINISHED DIGGING THE HOLE.

SHE'S OUT FOR THE POOR PIGEON NOW.

BEFORE SHE COULD RECOVER, THE PEACOCK AND THE PIGEON QUICKLY FLEW THROUGH THE DOOR...

...TO A TREE OUTSIDE.

THE CAT DASHED OUT AFTER THEM, BUT IT WAS TOO LATE.

SO BACK SHE WENT INTO THE HUT.

COME OUT, DEAR MOUSE. I'LL GIVE YOU GOLD. ALL THE GOLD I HAVE! AREN'T YOU MY NEPHEW?

OF COURSE! I AM YOUR NEPHEW! BUT I DON'T WANT YOUR GOLD.

8

JUST THEN A DOG ENTERED THE HUT.

WHAT ARE YOU UP TO, PUSS?

!

THE CAT PICKED UP THE CYMBALS...

...AND ADJUSTED HER EARTHEN ORNAMENT.

THEN —

BY THIS HOLY NECKLACE...

BUT THE DOG WAS NO FOOL.

WELL, WELL! A PIOUS CAT! MARVELLOUS!

WITH THAT HE SPRANG ON THE CAT...

...AND ATE HER.

LATER, WHEN THE DOG HAD LEFT, THE MOUSE CREPT OUT OF HIS HOLE.

ALL THAT WAS LEFT OF THE CAT WAS THE RIM OF THE BROKEN POT.

HE DRAGGED IT OUT OF THE HUT...

...AND SHOWED IT TO THE PEACOCK AND THE PIGEON.

LOOK, AUNTY HAS SENT YOU THIS RELIC OF LORD KEDAR.

A DOG CUT SHORT HER PILGRIMAGE BY BRINGING HER SALVATION RIGHT HERE!

HA! HA!

HA! HA!

NEVER AGAIN DID THE THREE FEEL THE URGE TO GO ON A PILGRIMAGE.

THE QUICK-WITTED FROG

ONE BRIGHT, SUNNY DAY, A FROG HOPPED OUT OF HIS POND TO TAKE A LOOK AT THE WORLD AROUND HIM.

HOW BEAUTIFUL IT IS OUT HERE!

I'LL HOP OVER TO THAT CLUMP OF BUSHES AND...

?

IT'S EVEN MORE BEAUTIFUL UP HERE IN THE ...

...HEAVENS! IT'S MY OLD ENEMY, THE CROW!

WHAT SHALL I DO? NOW. I SHALL CERTAINLY DIE!

BUT THEN IF DEATH IS A CERTAINTY, WHAT CAN I GAIN BY GIVING WAY TO DESPAIR?

HA! HA! OH, BROTHER CROW, IT'S ALL SO FUNNY!

YOU FOOL, YOU ARE ABOUT TO DIE AND YOU LAUGH!

IT IS YOU WHO ARE IN DANGER, MY FRIEND, NOT I. THE SNAKE WHO LIVES HERE IS BEHIND YOU, POISED TO KILL.

WITHOUT LOOKING BACK, THE CROW TOOK OFF WITH THE FROG.

ON AND ON HE FLEW.

AT LAST ——

HA! HA! HA!

LOOK BEHIND YOU. THE CAT, MY FOSTER SISTER, IS ABOUT TO POUNCE ON YOU.

THE FROG WAS BEGINNING TO ENJOY HIMSELF.

WHAT AN IDIOT THE CROW IS! AND TO THINK I WAS AFRAID OF HIM ALL THESE YEARS!

AFTER GETTING OVER HIS FRIGHT, THE CROW ALIGHTED ON AN IMAGE OF THE GODDESS KALI.

HA! HA! HA! HA!

I AM A DEVOTEE OF KALI AND SHE WILL NOT TOLERATE ANY HARM DONE TO ME HERE!

TREMBLING WITH FEAR, THE CROW ONCE AGAIN TOOK FLIGHT WITH THE FROG IN HIS BEAK.

BY NOW HE WAS TIRED AND THIRSTY. SO HE RETURNED TO THE POND.

HE EXPECTED TO HEAR THE USUAL HOARSE LAUGHTER FROM THE FROG, BUT THERE WAS SILENCE!

WHAT'S THIS? SO YOU HAVE NO FRIEND HERE TO HELP YOU!

NO, I AM ENTIRELY AT YOUR MERCY....

AHA!

"A Queen was kidnapped."

The King and his army went to her rescue.

If the **Ramayana** could be as simple as that,
it wouldn't have been an epic.

Get our latest product - **Tulsidas' Ramayana**
version of the Ramayana. Beautifully written and illustrated in
the classic style of Amar Chitra Katha comics, this hardbound
epic is a special volume with 160 pages.

To buy online, log on to **www.amarchitrakatha.com**

" When it comes to **STORIES**
UNCLE PAI knows best! "

For years you have let your imagination fly to
fantastic lands with Uncle Pai's stories.
Now he tells you which are his must-reads and why.
Log on to **www.amarchitrakatha.com** to buy
Uncle Pai's Favorite 50,
and get a personally autographed letter!

NOW AVAILABLE !
TINKLE SPECIAL COLLECTIONS

Price Rs 80 each

A COLLECTOR'S DELIGHT !

To buy online log on to **www.amarchitrakatha.com**

Call Toll free on **1800-233-9125** or SMS **'ACK BUY'** to **'575758'**

Who is growing **faster**? You or your Tinkle Digest collection?

With **220+** editions, and one new release **every month**, it's more likely to be Tinkle Digest.

TINKLE
Digest

Tinkle Magazine has been around since 1980. The best stories from 30 years of Tinkle starring your favorite Tinkle Toons, are republished in the Digest format.

NEVER AGAIN WILL I VENTURE OUT INTO THE OPEN!

MEANWHILE, THE CROW WAS HAPPILY SHARPENING HIS BEAK THINKING ONLY OF THE MEAL AWAITING HIM.

WHR WHR WHR

AH! MY BEAK IS SHARP NOW! COME, FRIEND!

BUT THERE WAS NO ANSWER! HE TURNED ROUND AND STILL DID NOT REALISE WHAT HAD HAPPENED.

COME, BROTHER FROG! MY BEAK IS SHARP NOW, SHARPER THAN A SWORD'S EDGE!

IS IT? GOOD. NOW YOU CAN START SHARPENING YOUR WITS.

A DEER STORY

A CART LADEN WITH HAY WAS BEING DRIVEN UP A FOREST PATH AT FULL SPEED, WHEN SUDDENLY —

OH! A DEER—RESTING RIGHT IN MY PATH!

HE JERKED THE REINS AND JUST MANAGED TO AVOID RUNNING OVER THE DEER.

DEAR SISTER, I CAN SEE YOU ARE NOT WELL. BUT PLEASE MOVE AND LET ME PASS.

BROTHER, I AM GOING TO BE A MOTHER. PLEASE HELP ME.

THE CARTER WAS A KIND-HEARTED MAN.

WHAT HELP DO YOU NEED, SISTER?

GIVE ME THAT CART-LOAD OF HAY TO KEEP MY YOUNG ONES WARM.

THE CARTER WAS TAKEN ABACK—

THE WHOLE CART-LOAD OF HAY! OH... WELL! ALL RIGHT, YOU CAN HAVE IT!

THANK YOU! I WILL PRAY THAT YOU AND YOUR CHILDREN PROSPER!

THE DEER IMMEDIATELY STARTED BUILDING HER HUT NEAR A FRAGRANT SAFFRON PLANT A FEW YARDS AWAY FROM THE ROAD.

THEN SHE WENT BACK TO THE PATH AND LAY DOWN THERE, QUITE TIRED AFTER ALL HER WORK.

SOON A CART LADEN WITH DOORS CAME HURTLING DOWN TOWARDS HER.

THIS CARTER TOO, JUST MANAGED TO STOP HIS CART IN TIME. HE WAS VERY ANGRY.

WHAT ARE YOU DOING IN THE MIDDLE OF THE PATH?

BROTHER, CAN'T YOU SEE I NEED HELP?

MY BABIES WILL SOON BE BORN. A GOOD MAN GAVE ME A CART-LOAD OF HAY TO BUILD A HUT BUT IT HAS NO DOOR.

YOU POOR DEER! I SHALL GIVE YOU A DOOR.

THE DEER FIXED THE DOOR IN PLACE AND SHUT IT.

THEN SHE WENT AND LAY DOWN IN HER USUAL PLACE. THIS TIME A CART LADEN WITH RICE AND JAGGERY CAME BY.

SHE TOLD THE DRIVER HER STORY.

...AND NOW, IF I HAD RICE AND JAGGERY TO PLASTER THE WALLS AND FLOOR, HOW COSY MY LITTLE HOUSE WOULD BE!

YOU SHALL HAVE THE RICE AND JAGGERY.

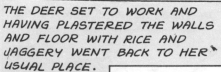

THE DEER SET TO WORK AND HAVING PLASTERED THE WALLS AND FLOOR WITH RICE AND JAGGERY WENT BACK TO HER USUAL PLACE.

WHO SHOULD COME BY NEXT BUT A CARTER WITH A CART-LOAD OF SUGAR, GHEE, DRIED GINGER, GUM AND ANISEED. JUST THE THINGS OUR DEER NEEDED!

...COULD YOU SPARE SOME OF THE THINGS YOU HAVE IN YOUR CART? FOR THEY ARE EATEN BY YOUNG MOTHERS AFTER CONFINEMENT.

WHY SOME, DEAR SISTER? I'LL GIVE YOU ENOUGH TO LAST YOU FOUR MONTHS.

THANK YOU! I WILL PRAY THAT YOU AND YOUR CHILDREN PROSPER!

THE DEER WAS NOW VERY HAPPY. ALTHOUGH SHE WAS ALONE IN THE WORLD AND LIVED IN THE MIDDLE OF A FOREST FAR FROM ALL HER RELATIVES, SHE HAD EVERYTHING SHE NEEDED.

SOON AFTER, FOUR LITTLE FAWNS WERE BORN.

FOR FORTY DAYS SHE STAYED WITH THEM IN THE HUT. SHE ATE THE FOOD SHE HAD STORED AND TENDERLY NURSED HER LITTLE ONES.

AT THE END OF THE FORTY DAYS SHE BATHED AND WORSHIPPED THE SUN.

THEN SHE TURNED TO HER CHILDREN.

MY CHILDREN, I MUST GO OUT TO GRAZE. OTHERWISE, I'LL BECOME WEAK AND ILL. AND THEN WHO WILL FEED YOU?

SO LISTEN TO ME CAREFULLY. DON'T LET ANYONE COME IN WHEN I AM AWAY, AND ALL WILL BE WELL.

WE WILL BE VERY CAREFUL, MOTHER. WE WON'T OPEN THE DOOR TO ANYONE BUT YOU.

JUST THEN A LAME WOLF HAPPENED TO PASS BY.

HM! LOVELY LITTLE ONES...

AHH.... SHE HAS GONE! GOOD!

WHO IS THERE?

THE WOLF DARED NOT REPLY. SO HE KNOCKED AGAIN.

YOU CAN'T BE OUR MOTHER. GO AWAY.

THEY THINK THEY'RE TOO SMART. H-M-M. WE'LL SEE.

26

IN THE EVENING, HE HID IN THE BUSHES AND AWAITED THE MOTHER'S RETURN.

MY SWEET LITTLE ONES, IN THE HUT PLASTERED WITH JAGGERY DECORATED WITH RICE, OPEN THE DOOR TO YOUR MOTHER.

THEY OPENED THE DOOR IMMEDIATELY.

SO HAPPY WERE THEY TO SEE HER THAT THEY FORGOT TO TELL HER OF THE EARLIER VISITOR.

THE NEXT MORNING —

AHH... SHE'S LEAVING.

HE WAITED FOR A WHILE AND THEN WENT UP TO THE DOOR.

MY SWEET LITTLE ONES, IN THE HUT PLASTERED WITH JAGGERY DECORATED WITH RICE, OPEN THE DOOR TO YOUR MOTHER.

THE CHILDREN WERE ABOUT TO OPEN THE DOOR WHEN SUDDENLY A SWEET, MELODIOUS VOICE CALLED OUT A WARNING.

DON'T, CHILDREN! DON'T OPEN THE DOOR! IT'S THE LAME WOLF OUTSIDE, NOT YOUR MOTHER!

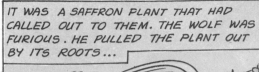

IT WAS A SAFFRON PLANT THAT HAD CALLED OUT TO THEM. THE WOLF WAS FURIOUS. HE PULLED THE PLANT OUT BY ITS ROOTS...

...AND WENT BACK TO THE DOOR.

MY SWEET LITTLE ONES, IN THE HUT PLASTERED WITH JAGGERY DECORATED WITH RICE, OPEN THE DOOR TO YOUR MOTHER.

AGAIN, THEY WERE ABOUT TO OPEN THE DOOR WHEN —

DON'T, CHILDREN, DON'T! IT'S ONLY THE BAD, LAME WOLF!

YOU...!

SEETHING WITH RAGE THE WOLF BURNT THE SAFFRON PLANT, MIXED THE ASHES WITH WATER AND DRANK UP THE MIXTURE.

MEANWHILE, INSIDE THE HUT —

I WISH MOTHER WOULD COME SOON!

A FEW MINUTES LATER —

MY SWEET LITTLE ONES, I....

THAT VOICE AGAIN!

ISN'T THAT MOTHER?

LET'S OPEN THE DOOR FOR HER.

NO! LET'S WAIT A WHILE! IF IT'S THE BAD WOLF, THE SAFFRON PLANT WILL WARN US AGAIN.

THEY WAITED FOR A WHILE. THEN—

THE SAFFRON PLANT IS QUIET. IT MUST BE MOTHER.

LET'S OPEN THE DOOR!

THEY OPENED THE DOOR...

...AND THERE STOOD THE LAME WOLF.

IN THE EVENING, WHEN THE MOTHER DEER CAME HOME—

THE SAFFRON PLANT... WHERE HAS IT DISAPPEARED?

THE DOOR IS WIDE OPEN. MY BABIES! WHERE ARE MY BABIES?

SHE RAN OUT OF THE HUT TO LOOK FOR THEM.

WOLF-TRACKS! THE LAME WOLF MUST HAVE CARRIED THEM AWAY.

CRYING LOUDLY, SHE FOLLOWED THE TRACKS.

AIE! AIE!

HE HAD NOT GONE FAR. HE WAS DOWN BY THE WATER'S EDGE.

OH, CRUEL WOLF! GIVE ME BACK MY CHILDREN!

OH! YOU! I'LL EAT YOU TOO!

AND HE SPRANG TOWARDS HER.

BUT—

AS HE FELL, HIS STOMACH BURST OPEN AND ...

...OUT POPPED THE FOUR PRETTY, YOUNG FAWNS AND A FRESH GREEN SAFFRON PLANT.

MOTHER!

MOTHER!

THE DEER TENDERLY BATHED AND FED THEM AND TOOK THEM HOME.

SHE PLANTED THE SAFFRON IN ITS OLD PLACE.

AND EVERY DAY SHE WATERED IT WITH SWEETENED MILK.

AS FOR THE WICKED, LAME WOLF, HE WAS NEVER HEARD OF AGAIN.

PLAY, CREATE and SHARE on www.TinkleOnline.com

Play games with your favourite Tinkle Toons – Suppandi & Shikari Shambu. Solve fun-filled puzzles, quizzes and more.

Create your own avatars, write stories & draw toons!

Share stories, fun facts and exchange virtual gifts with your friends.

www.TinkleOnline.com – India's first fully-moderated destination site for kids

THE PIG
AND THE DOG

AND OTHER ANIMAL TALES FROM ARUNACHAL PRADESH

www.amarchitrakatha.com

The route to your roots

THE PIG AND THE DOG

Why are dogs kept in the house as pets, while pigs must stay outside?

This collection of folk tales from Arunachal Pradesh has ingenious and hilarious explanations for all kinds of phenomena, from why langurs have black faces, to why tigers have stripes.

In the hills of Arunachal Pradesh, as the family gathers before dinner, grandmothers and grandfathers answer the children's questions with age-old legends and stories. Arunachal Pradesh has a rich culture of folktales that are told and re-told, shared across generations and tribes. The story of the pig and the dog is from the Adi tribe while the story of the monkey is popular in the Nocte tribe.

Script
Luis Fernandes

Illustrations
Ram Waeerkar

Editor
Anant Pai

THE PIG AND THE DOG

A MAN HAD A PIG AND A DOG.

ONE DAY HE SUDDENLY REALISED THAT THE TWO ANIMALS DID NO WORK AT ALL.

GET UP, YOU LAZY CREATURES!

GO AND DO SOMETHING USEFUL!

WHICHEVER OF YOU DOES SOME WORK MIGHT FIND A PLACE IN MY HOUSE.

THE PIG AND THE DOG WENT TO THEIR MASTER'S FIELD.

THERE THE PIG PLOUGHED THE FIELD THE WHOLE DAY LONG...

...WHILE THE DOG SLEPT.

IN THE EVENING —

HAVE YOU FINISHED?

YES... AND I AM EXHAUSTED.

AS THE PIG WEARILY SET OFF FOR HOME, THE DOG JUMPED INTO THE FIELD...

...RAN UP AND DOWN SEVERAL TIMES ...

...AND THEN FOLLOWED HIM.

THAT NIGHT —

WHAT WORK DID YOU DO TODAY?

I PLOUGHED THE FIELD, MASTER.

AND YOU?

MASTER...

...IT WAS I WHO PLOUGHED THE FIELD.

2

I WILL HAVE TO FIND OUT THE TRUTH FOR MYSELF.

THE MAN GOT UP EARLY NEXT MORNING AND WENT TO THE FIELD. WHEN HE RETURNED —

ARE YOU SATISFIED WITH MY WORK, MASTER?

WHAT WORK?

I PLOUGHED YOUR FIELD.

YOU LIAR!

I SAW ONLY THE DOG'S FOOTPRINTS IN THE SOIL. IT WAS HE WHO PLOUGHED THE FIELD.

BUT... BUT...

GO AWAY, YOU LAZY CREATURE.

COME, DOG. YOU HAVE DONE SOME HARD WORK. YOU MAY COME INTO THE HOUSE WITH ME.

EVER SINCE DOGS HAVE STAYED IN THEIR MASTERS' HOUSES AND PIGS HAVE NOT BEEN ALLOWED INSIDE.

THE OWL AND THE TIGER

ONE DAY THE BIRDS AND ANIMALS OF THE EARTH HELD A MEETING...

...AT WHICH THEY CHOSE THE TIGER TO BE KING OF THE JUNGLE...

...AND THE OWL TO BE HIS MINISTER.

BUT THE KING AND HIS MINISTER HAD QUITE DIFFERENT NATURES. THE TIGER WAS RASH...

...AND THE OWL WAS PROUD.

ONE DAY THEY HAD AN ARGUMENT...

...WHICH TURNED INTO A QUARREL. THE ANGRY TIGER SLAPPED THE OWL SO HARD...

...THAT THE OWL'S FACE BECAME FLAT!

THE ANGRY BIRD PICKED UP A BURNING LOG...

...AND STRUCK THE TIGER WITH IT, LEAVING LONG BLACK STRIPES ON ITS BODY.

SINCE THAT DAY OWLS HAVE FLAT FACES AND TIGERS BLACK STRIPES ON THEIR BODIES.

WHY CRABS HAVE FLAT BODIES

THERE ONCE LIVED A CRAB NEAR A RIVER. ONE DAY AS HE WAS LOOKING LONGINGLY AT THE FRUIT ON A TALL TREE, HIS FRIEND THE MOUSE CAME ALONG.

WOULD YOU LIKE TO EAT SOME OF THOSE FRUIT?

I WOULD LOVE TO.

I'LL CLIMB UP AND THROW SOME DOWN FOR YOU.

THE MOUSE CLIMBED THE TREE...

...AND BEGAN TO THROW THE FRUIT DOWN.

ONE OF THEM HIT A NEST OF RED ANTS.

THUD

THE ANTS GOT FURIOUS AND RUSHED OUT OF THEIR NEST.

WHO DID THAT?

IT MUST BE THAT BOAR!

6

I AM SORRY... BUT THERE'S A BAT IN MY EAR.

SEE! THERE IT IS!

I WAS TRYING TO GET AWAY FROM A BOAR.

HE KNOCKED DOWN THE TREE IN WHICH I WAS SLEEPING.

LET'S FIND HIM.

WHEN THEY FOUND THE BOAR —

I AM HOMELESS BECAUSE OF YOU. YOU FRIGHTENED THE BAT AND HE FRIGHTENED THE ELEPHANT AND HE KNOCKED DOWN MY HOUSE.

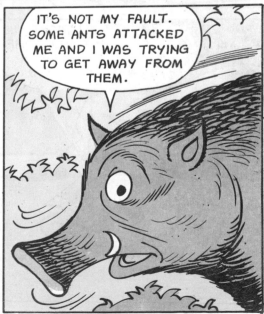

IT'S NOT MY FAULT. SOME ANTS ATTACKED ME AND I WAS TRYING TO GET AWAY FROM THEM.

9

WHEN THE OLD WOMAN QUESTIONED THE ANTS —

WE HAD GOOD REASON TO ATTACK HIM. HE BROKE OUR NEST.

I DIDN'T.

A MOUSE WAS THROWING THAT CRAB SOME FRUIT AND ONE OF THEM HIT THE NEST.

WHEN THE CRAB WAS QUESTIONED —

I...ER...YES. ONE OF THE FRUIT DID HIT THE NEST.

SO YOU ARE TO BE BLAMED FOR THE DESTRUCTION OF MY HUT. YOU'LL HAVE TO GIVE ME SOMETHING TO MAKE UP FOR IT.

SHE IS RIGHT.

ALL RIGHT. I'LL GET YOU SOMETHING FROM MY HOUSE.

THE CRAB CREPT UNDER A STONE...

...AND STAYED THERE.

COME OUT! COME OUT!

FINALLY THE WOMAN AND THE ANIMALS GOT VERY ANGRY.

LET'S PRESS THE ROCK DOWN ON HIM.

OH-OH!

HELP!

THAT'S ENOUGH!

THE OLD WOMAN AND THE ANIMALS WENT AWAY.

SOMETIME LATER THE CRAB CRAWLED OUT FROM UNDER THE ROCK BUT HE HAD BECOME AS FLAT AS A PANCAKE.

CRABS EVER SINCE HAVE HAD FLAT BODIES.

THE OTTER AND THE WILDCAT

AN OTTER AND A WILDCAT HAD BECOME FRIENDS. ONE DAY THE OTTER ACCOMPANIED THE CAT TO A VILLAGE.

I'LL STEAL A CHICKEN FOR YOU AND ONE FOR ME...

...BUT KEEP AN EYE OUT FOR MEN. SHOUT A WARNING IF YOU SEE ANY OF THEM COMING TOWARDS ME.

THE CAT CREPT INTO A HUT...

...AND CAUGHT A FOWL.

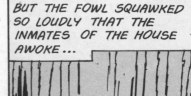

BUT THE FOWL SQUAWKED SO LOUDLY THAT THE INMATES OF THE HOUSE AWOKE...

...AND BEGAN TO CHASE THE CAT.

THE OTTER WHO WAS WATCHING WAS TERRIFIED.

AFTER THOSE PEOPLE CATCH HIM, THEY'LL COME AFTER ME.

I'D BETTER GET OUT OF HERE.

AND THE OTTER RAN AWAY AS FAST AS HE COULD.

BUT THE CAT GOT AWAY FROM HIS PURSUERS AND CAUGHT UP WITH THE OTTER.

YOU COWARD!

I...I AM SORRY.

I AM NOT USED TO THIS SORT OF THING.

THE CAT ATE THE FOWL...

...AND THREW THE BONES TO THE OTTER.

THERE, THAT'S YOUR SHARE.

THE OTTER FELT HURT BUT DID NOT SAY ANYTHING.

SOME DAYS LATER AS THEY WERE PASSING BY A POND —

LET'S CATCH SOME FISH.

BUT I CAN'T SWIM.

YOU GO INTO THE POND, CATCH THE FISH AND THROW THEM TO ME.

THE OTTER DIVED INTO THE POND...

...CAUGHT AND ATE SEVERAL FISH...

...AND THREW THE BONES TO THE CAT.

THERE! THAT'S YOUR SHARE.

YOU RASCAL! I'LL TEAR YOU APART.

IN HIS ANGER THE CAT FORGOT THAT HE DID NOT KNOW HOW TO SWIM. HE JUMPED INTO THE WATER TO CATCH THE OTTER...

...AND WAS DROWNED.

THE BULBUL AND THE HORNBILL

THE HORNBILL WAS ONCE THE KING OF THE BIRDS. BUT HE USED TO KILL SMALLER BIRDS IF THEY MADE THE SLIGHTEST MISTAKE.

SO ONE DAY ALL THE BIRDS GOT TOGETHER AND DECIDED THAT THEY MUST HAVE A NEW KING. THEIR CHOICE FELL ON THE BULBUL.

HE HAS A REGAL APPEARANCE...

...AND HE COULD NOT HURT ANYONE EVEN IF HE WANTED TO.

BUT HOW DO WE BREAK THE NEWS TO THE HORNBILL? HE WON'T BE PLEASED.

I HAVE AN IDEA.

I'LL NEED YOUR HELP, WOODPECKER. COME WITH ME.

SOMETIME LATER—

O KING, WE FEEL THAT YOU SHOULD UNDERGO A TEST AND PROVE YOUR WORTH. YOU WILL HAVE TO SIT ON A THICK BRANCH AND BREAK IT.

IF YOU DON'T SUCCEED, WHOEVER DOES SHALL BE DEEMED WORTHIER OF RULING US.

TELL ME WHICH BRANCH I SHOULD SIT ON.

THAT'S THE BRANCH.

IF I CANNOT BREAK THE BRANCH WHO CAN?

THE HORNBILL FLEW UP TO IT...

...AND LANDED ON IT WITH ALL HIS MIGHT.

BUT THE BRANCH DID NOT BREAK.

REMEMBER, ANYONE WHO ENTERS THE CONTEST MUST SIT ON AN EQUALLY THICK BRANCH.

THE BULBUL IS THE NEXT CONTESTANT. IS THE BRANCH OVER THERE THICK ENOUGH?

THAT BRANCH IS EVEN THICKER THAN THIS.

IF THE BULBUL CAN BREAK THAT BRANCH HE CERTAINLY DESERVES TO BE KING.

GO ON!

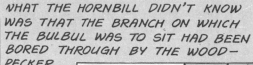

WHAT THE HORNBILL DIDN'T KNOW WAS THAT THE BRANCH ON WHICH THE BULBUL WAS TO SIT HAD BEEN BORED THROUGH BY THE WOODPECKER.

AND WHEN THE BULBUL LANDED ON IT —

CRACK

HE...HE HAS BROKEN THE BRANCH.

THE HORNBILL ACKNOWLEDGING DEFEAT FLEW AWAY.

AND THE BULBUL BECAME KING OF THE BIRDS.

17

THE PORCUPINE AND THE ELEPHANTS

A HERD OF ELEPHANTS USED TO BATHE IN A PARTICULAR POOL IN THE JUNGLE. ONE DAY—

WHY IS OUR POOL SO MUDDY TODAY?

SOMEBODY HAS BEEN PLAYING IN THE WATER.

WHO?

DRAGONFLY, DO YOU KNOW WHO HAS DIRTIED OUR POOL.

NO!

IF YOU FIND THE CULPRIT LET US KNOW.

SOMETIME LATER THE DRAGONFLY SAW A PORCUPINE.

DID YOU BY ANY CHANCE BATHE IN THE POOL THE ELEPHANTS USE?

I DID.

THEY ARE ANNOYED BECAUSE YOU MADE IT SO MUDDY.

I CAN'T HELP IT IF THERE'S SO MUCH MUD IN THAT POOL.

ANYWAY THAT POOL DOESN'T BELONG TO THEM. I'LL USE IT WHENEVER I WANT TO.

THE DRAGONFLY WENT BACK TO THE ELEPHANTS.

I HAVE FOUND THE ANIMAL THAT MUDDIED YOUR POOL.

HE IS NOT AT ALL REPENTANT. HE SAYS HE WILL USE THIS POOL AGAIN.

HE DOESN'T KNOW WHO HE IS DEALING WITH.

THE LEADER OF THE HERD PLUCKED A HAIR FROM HIS HEAD AND GAVE IT TO THE DRAGONFLY.

SHOW THIS TO THAT STUPID CREATURE.

TELL HIM HE IS PICKING UP A QUARREL WITH ONE WHOSE HAIR IS SO THICK.

THE DRAGONFLY TOOK THE HAIR TO PORCUPINE.

THE ELEPHANTS SAY YOU DO NOT KNOW WHOM YOU ARE DEALING WITH.

EACH HAIR OF THEIRS IS SO THICK.

YOU CALL THAT THICK?

HERE, TAKE ONE OF MINE TO THEM.

THE DRAGONFLY TOOK THE PORCUPINE'S QUILL TO THE ELEPHANTS.

HE HAS SENT YOU A HAIR OF HIS OWN.

WHAT!

IS EACH HAIR OF HIS SO THICK?

HE MUST BE A GIANT OF A CREATURE.

LET'S NOT QUARREL WITH HIM, BROTHERS. WE'LL FIND ANOTHER POOL TOMORROW.

THE ELEPHANTS SCRAMBLED OUT OF THE POOL AND RAN AWAY.

20

THE FROG AND THE MONKEY

LONG AGO THERE WAS A RAJA. HE HAD A MONKEY AND A FROG AS HIS SERVANTS. ONE DAY —

GO TO THE FOREST AND BRING ME SOME FRUIT.

AND YOU GET ME SOME FISH FROM THE STREAM.

THE FROG AND THE MONKEY SET OUT TO DO THEIR MASTER'S BIDDING.

BUT WHEN THEY REACHED THE FOREST, THE MONKEY ATE EVERY FRUIT HE PICKED.

AND WHEN HIS STOMACH WAS FULL...

...HE CURLED UP ON A TREE AND WENT TO SLEEP.

HE AWOKE ONLY TOWARDS EVENING. AND THEN HE WAS AFRAID TO GO HOME.

THE RAJA WILL BEAT ME FOR NOT BRINGING HIM FRUITS.

NOW WHAT SHOULD I DO?

FINALLY HE GOT OFF THE TREE, ROLLED IN THE MUD SEVERAL TIMES ...

... AND SET OFF FOR HOME.

ON THE WAY HE MET THE FROG. THE FROG HAD WORKED HARD AND CAUGHT A LOT OF FISH.

THIS CREATURE WILL GET ME INTO TROUBLE.

WHY DID HE HAVE TO CATCH SO MANY FISH? AND I DON'T HAVE SO MUCH AS A BERRY TO GIVE THE RAJA.

THIS WON'T DO AT ALL!

HEY! WHAT ARE YOU DOING?

SEE WHAT YOU'VE DONE! I'VE LOST ALL THE FISH!

IT DOESN'T MATTER.

WHY ARE YOU SO AFRAID OF THE RAJA? HE WON'T REMAIN OUR MASTER MUCH LONGER YOU KNOW.

WHAT DO YOU MEAN?

I'M GOING TO REBEL AGAINST HIM.

OH!

AND WHEN I BECOME THE NEW RAJA, I'LL MAKE YOU MY MINISTER.

NOW COME, LET'S GO HOME. TELL HIM YOU DIDN'T CATCH ANY FISH.

THE RAJA WAS VERY ANGRY WHEN HE SAW THE SERVANTS RETURNING EMPTY-HANDED.

WHAT COULD I DO, MASTER? I SCOURED THE WHOLE JUNGLE FOR FRUIT-BEARING TREES...

...BUT I COULD NOT FIND ANY. SEE HOW DIRTY AND DISHEVELLED I AM. DOES THAT NOT SHOW THAT I HAVE BEEN WORKING?

HE, ON THE OTHER HAND LOOKS SO CLEAN AND FRESH.

HE MUST HAVE SPENT THE WHOLE DAY PLAYING IN THE WATER.

YOU KNOW THAT'S NOT TRUE!

YOU USELESS CREATURE!

THE RAJA HIT HIM SO HARD...

...THAT THE TOP OF HIS HEAD BECAME FLAT.

I SENT YOU TO CATCH FISH, NOT TO PLAY IN THE WATER!

I DID CATCH FISH.

BUT HE THREW ALL OF THEM INTO THE STREAM!

I CAN'T STAY HERE ANY MORE. THERE'S NO JUSTICE HERE.

THE FROG LEFT THE PALACE AND WENT TO LIVE IN THE RIVER. BUT FROGS SINCE THEN HAVE FLAT HEADS.

THE MONKEY WAS GLAD TO GET RID OF THE FROG. A FEW DAYS LATER HE REBELLED AGAINST THE RAJA.

MASTER, HE IS COMING TO ATTACK YOU WITH HIS RELATIVES.

THE TRAITOR!

I MUST ACT FAST IF I AM TO SAVE MYSELF.

THE RAJA MADE A BLACK PASTE...

...AND COVERED HIS FACE WITH IT.

THEN HE WAITED FOR THE MONKEYS TO APPEAR. AFTER SOME TIME —

HE'S COMING ALONE. HE WANTS TO SEE HOW WELL PRE- PARED I AM.

?

WELL?

WHERE DID YOU GET THAT PASTE, MASTER? I WOULD LIKE TO PUT SOME ON MY FACE TOO.

MY SERVANTS PUT ME IN THE HOLLOW OF A LARGE TREE AND LIT A FIRE AROUND IT.

THE SMOKE MADE MY FACE BLACK.

IT LOOKS BEAUTIFUL NOW.

PLEASE ASK YOUR SERVANTS TO DO THE SAME THING FOR ME, AND MY FRIENDS.

GLADLY.

THE RAJA'S SERVANTS PUT THE MONKEY AND HIS FRIENDS IN THE HOLLOW OF A LARGE TREE...

...AND SET FIRE TO IT.

ONLY ONE OF THE MONKEYS ESCAPED. THE ONE WHO ESCAPED WAS A FEMALE AND HER FACE HAD BECOME BLACK WITH SMOKE.

HER DESCENDANTS ARE THE BLACK-FACED MONKEYS, WE SEE TODAY.

THE FROG AND THE TIGER

A FROG AND A TIGER WERE FRIENDS. THE FROG WAS A FREQUENT VISITOR AT THE TIGER'S HOUSE. AND WHEN- EVER HE CAME, THE TIGER GAVE HIM MEAT TO EAT.

ONE DAY—

I HAVE COME TO YOUR HOUSE SO OFTEN. BUT YOU HAVE NEVER COME TO MINE.

PLEASE COME TO MY HOUSE TOMORROW.

I WOULD BE DELIGHTED TO COME. BUT...

...I AM A MEAT-EATER.

AS IF THERE'S NO MEAT IN MY HOUSE!

PLEASE DO COME.

OH, ALL RIGHT.

THE FROG WENT HOME FEELING RATHER WORRIED.

WHAT HAVE I GONE AND DONE!

THUMP

OUCH! BOTH MY LEGS MUST BE BROKEN.

THE FROG DRAGGED HIMSELF HOME.

THE NEXT DAY WHEN THE TIGER CAME—

WELCOME, MY FRIEND, WELCOME!

PLEASE MAKE YOURSELF AT HOME WHILE I GET YOU SOMETHING TO EAT.

THE FROG HOPPED UP TO THE LOFT.

AFTER SOME TIME—

OOOOOOH!

WHAT IS HE DOING?

WHAT ARE YOU DOING, MY FRIEND? WHY ARE YOU BITING OFF FLESH FROM YOUR LEG.

I...UH...

I HAD NO MEAT TO OFFER YOU...

...SO YOU WANTED TO GIVE ME YOUR OWN FLESH?

DO YOU THINK I WOULD HAVE EATEN IT? WHY DID YOU DO SUCH A THING?

THE FROG FELT VERY ASHAMED OF HIMSELF.

WHEN THE TIGER LEFT...

...HE HOPPED TO THE RIVER...

...AND JUMPED INTO IT.

I COULD NEVER SHOW MY FACE TO THE TIGER AGAIN. I SHALL STAY IN THE WATER FOR THE REST OF MY LIFE.

FROGS TO THIS DAY LIVE IN THE WATER.

NOW AVAILABLE !
TINKLE SPECIAL COLLECTIONS

Price Rs 80 each

A COLLECTOR'S DELIGHT !

To buy online log on to **www.amarchitrakatha.com**

Call Toll free on **1800-233-9125** or SMS **'ACK BUY'** to **'575758'**

FRIENDS AND FOES

ANIMAL TALES FROM THE MAHABHARATA

www.amarchitrakatha.com

The route to your roots

FRIENDS AND FOES

In the Mahabharata, when Yudhishthira asks Bheeshma what the right conduct of a king should be, the wise Bheeshma answers in the form of stories. Cats and mice, crows and swans, leopards and jackals, all serve to show how a king must deal in times of crisis, doubt or personal problems.

Script	**Illustrations**	**Editor**
Toni Patel	Pradeep Sathe	Anant Pai

FRIENDS AND FOES

IN THE DEPTHS OF A FOREST, THERE WAS A LARGE BANYAN TREE. IN A HOLE, AT THE FOOT OF THIS TREE, LIVED A RAT NAMED PALITA.

AMIDST THE BRANCHES OF THE SAME TREE THERE DWELT A CAT CALLED LOMASHA AND PALITA WAS IN CONSTANT FEAR OF HIM.

LOMASHA MUST STILL BE UP THERE. I HAD BETTER STAY HERE TILL HE LEAVES.

AH! I CAN SEE LOMASHA NOW! EVERY DAY HE DEVOURS SO MANY OF THOSE POOR BIRDS!

GOOD! A PLUMP MOUTHFUL!

THANK GOD, LOMASHA IS BUSY! NOW I CAN SNEAK OUT AND GET SOMETHING TO EAT!

ONE DAY, A HUNTER CAME TO STAY IN THE FOREST.

EACH DAY, HE WOULD SPREAD OUT HIS NET AT SUNSET...

...AND COME BACK AT DAWN THE NEXT DAY TO CHECK IF AN ANIMAL HAD BEEN TRAPPED.

AH! A DEER THIS TIME!

LOMASHA WAS CAREFUL TO KEEP AWAY FROM THE NET. BUT, ONE DAY —

OH, THIS IS TERRIBLE! THE MORE I STRUGGLE, THE MORE FIRMLY I AM TRAPPED!

THIS IS MY LUCKY DAY! MY ARCH-ENEMY HAS BEEN CAUGHT. I CAN GO ABOUT FREELY NOW!

WITH LOMASHA FIRMLY IN THE NET, PALITA BECAME VERY BOLD.

HA! HA! DEAR LOMASHA! YOU HAVE NO IDEA HOW HAPPY I AM!

WHAT JOY! THIS IS THE GREATEST DAY OF MY LIFE!

ENJOYING HIS NEW-FOUND FREEDOM, PALITA JUMPED ABOUT NEAR THE VERY SNARE WHICH HELD THE CAT PRISONER.

BUT HIS JOY WAS SHORT-LIVED. SUDDENLY HIS EYE FELL UPON A NEW DANGER — THE ARRIVAL OF A TERRIBLE FOE!

OH! A MONGOOSE!

HE LOOKED AROUND FOR A WAY TO ESCAPE AND GOT ANOTHER SHOCK—THERE WAS AN OWL ON THE TREE!

WHAT SHALL I DO?

IF I STAY HERE, THAT OWL WILL TEAR ME TO PIECES WITH HIS SHARP BEAK...

...BUT IF I TRY TO RUN AWAY THE MONGOOSE WILL SWALLOW ME UP!

ON EVERY SIDE THERE IS DANGER! DEATH ITSELF IS STARING ME IN THE FACE!

I THOUGHT I WAS LUCKY WHEN MY WORST ENEMY, LOMASHA, WAS ENSNARED. BUT, IN A WAY, HE PROTECTED ME FROM THE OTHERS BY HIS VERY PRESENCE.

AND NOW HE COULD DO WITH MY HELP... THAT'S IT! HE NEEDS ME AND I NEED HIM.

TURNING TO THE CAT, HE TALKED TO HIM WITH FRIENDLY CONCERN.

DEAR LOMASHA, I WISH TO HELP YOU. IF YOU AGREE TO DO THE SAME FOR ME, I WILL RELEASE YOU FROM YOUR PRESENT PLIGHT. WILL YOU LISTEN TO ME?

DO YOU REALLY MEAN TO HELP ME? A SHORT WHILE AGO YOU WERE REJOICING AT MY MISFORTUNE!

THINGS ARE DIFFERENT NOW. I THOUGHT OF YOU AS MY ONLY ENEMY BUT I HAD FORGOTTEN ABOUT THE MONGOOSE AND THE OWL.

LOOK, THERE THEY ARE, WAITING TO POUNCE UPON ME!

5

YES, INDEED, IT'S TRUE. BUT HOW CAN I HELP YOU, BOUND AS I AM BY THE HUNTER'S NET?

FRIEND, THE ANSWER IS VERY SIMPLE: LET ME LIE CROUCHED UNDER YOUR BODY TILL THEY LEAVE!

OH! I SEE! AND WHEN THEY LEAVE, YOU WILL RELEASE ME!

YOU ARE QUICK TO UNDERSTAND, O WISE CAT! SO YOU AGREE?

OF COURSE, LOMASHA AGREED.

PALITA QUICKLY SNUGGLED UP TO THE CAT. THE CAT DID NOT MOVE, BUT LAY VERY STILL.

ISN'T IT EXTRAORDINARY? I DON'T EVEN THINK OF PALITA AS A RAT! HE IS MY SAVIOUR!

WHAT A STRANGE TURN OF EVENTS! I ACTUALLY FEEL SAFE UNDER THE BODY OF LOMASHA, THE CAT!

MEANWHILE, THE MONGOOSE HAD HIS EYES FIXED ON PALITA.

A RAT IN THE ARMS OF A CAT! I'VE NEVER SEEN ANYTHING LIKE IT IN MY LIFE!

ANYWAY, I CAN'T WAIT HERE FOREVER. I'LL FIND SOMETHING ELSE TO EAT!

GOOD! HE'S GOING AWAY!

PRETTY SOON THE OWL, TOO, GAVE UP.

IT WILL SOON BE DAYBREAK..I'D BETTER LOOK FOR ANOTHER PREY!

AFTER THIS, PALITA BEGAN TO CUT THE STRINGS OF THE NET WITH HIS SHARP TEETH.

O, WISE BEING! THROUGH YOUR GRACE, I HAVE ALMOST GOT BACK MY LIFE!

BUT PALITA, IN ACCORDANCE WITH HIS OWN PLANS, WORKED VERY SLOWLY.

DEAR FRIEND, DON'T WASTE TIME. DO CUT THESE STRINGS QUICKLY! IT WILL SOON BE DAWN AND THE HUNTER WILL BE HERE!

PATIENCE! ALL IN GOOD TIME!

PALITA CONTINUED TO WORK SLOWLY WHILE LOMASHA WAITED TREMBLING WITH FEAR.

I SEE A RED GLOW IN THE EAST. SOON IT WILL BE DAWN. OH, DO HURRY!

PATIENCE, FRIEND, PATIENCE!

WHEN, AT LAST, THE SUN ROSE IN THE EAST —

SEE, THE HUNTER IS APPROACHING! NOW I WILL SET YOU FREE!

PALITA CUT THE LAST STRINGS THAT HELD LOMASHA, JUST AS THE HUNTER REACHED THE SCENE.

THERE! YOU SEE, I HAVE KEPT MY WORD!

THE CAT BOUNDED AWAY...

...WHILE THE RAT QUICKLY LEAPED TO HIS HOLE.

WHAT'S THIS? MY SNARE TORN TO BITS AND NO ANIMAL IN SIGHT?

WHEN THE PUZZLED HUNTER HAD GONE AWAY, THE CAT ADDRESSED HIS NEW-FOUND FRIEND.

OH, PALITA, I AM VERY GRATEFUL TO YOU FOR SAVING MY LIFE! LET THERE BE PEACE BETWEEN US ALWAYS! I WILL ASK ALL MY KINSMEN AND FRIENDS NOT TO HURT YOU.

BUT THE RAT WAS WISE.

YOU ARE MISTAKEN, O LOMASHA! THERE ARE TIMES WHEN SELF-INTEREST CAN MAKE A FOE A FRIEND. BUT SOONER OR LATER THEY WILL BECOME ENEMIES.

NO, NO. NOT IF ONE OF THEM HAS SAVED THE OTHER'S LIFE!

IT IS POSSIBLE YOU ARE PRETENDING TO BE MY FRIEND — JUST TO CATCH ME THE MORE EASILY!

PLEASE, LISTEN TO ME···

NO, LOMASHA, GO YOUR WAY — AND KEEP YOUR DISTANCE FROM THE *EVIL* HUNTER!

THE CAT SHIVERED ON HEARING THE WORD 'HUNTER' AND MADE HASTE TO RUN AWAY.

THE TIGER AND THE JACKAL

DEEP IN THE JUNGLES OF THE HIMALAYAS, THERE WAS A JACKAL WHO LIVED THE LIFE OF A RECLUSE.

THIS JACKAL WAS COMPASSIONATE AND TRUTHFUL WHEREAS HIS COMPANIONS WERE CRUEL AND RAPACIOUS.

WHAT STRANGE BEHAVIOUR IS THIS? ONE WOULD THINK HE WAS AN ASCETIC PRACTISING AUSTERITIES!

AND WE JACKALS RELISH FLESH.

SUCH BEHAVIOUR IS PERVERSE! EVERY ONE MUST REMAIN TRUE TO HIS NATURE!

LET'S GO AND GIVE HIM A BIT OF ADVICE.

LOOK, FRIEND, THE WAY IN WHICH YOU LIVE WON'T DO! WE DON'T LIKE IT!

ALL OF US WILL GIVE YOU MEAT. YOU DON'T HAVE TO LIVE LIKE AN ASCETIC!

THANK YOU FOR YOUR KIND CONCERN, BUT I AM QUITE HAPPY LIVING ON FRUIT.

HA! DO YOU IMAGINE THAT BY IMITATING A HIGHER CASTE YOU CAN CHANGE YOUR POSITION IN SOCIETY?

10

IT'S TRUE I AM LOW-BORN BUT I AM DETERMINED THAT MY CONDUCT SHALL NOT BE LOW.

SO YOU BELIEVE IT IS UP TO YOU TO DECIDE ON YOUR CONDUCT?

DON'T YOU REALISE IT HAS ALL BEEN LAID DOWN FOR US GENERATIONS AGO? WE JACKALS HAVE STRICTLY FOLLOWED THE SAME RULES AS OUR FATHERS!

FRIENDS, SINCE WE ARE RESPONSIBLE FOR OUR ACTIONS DOES IT NOT FOLLOW THAT WE HAVE A CHOICE OVER OUR ACTIONS?

HE SEEMS TO BE A TRULY LEARNED PERSON OF BLAMELESS CONDUCT.

I DO NOT WISH TO LEAD YOUR KIND OF LIFE. IT IS EVIL. IT LEADS TO DISCONTENT AND TEMPTATION.

PAH! IT'S NO USE TALKING TO HIM! LET'S LEAVE HIM ALONE!

SUCH SUPERIOR AIRS!

MOST UNUSUAL FOR A JACKAL! HE IS WORTHY OF RESPECT!

11

THE TIGER WHO WAS EAVESDROPPING WAS THE KING OF THE FOREST. HE DREW NEAR AS SOON AS THE OTHERS HAD LEFT.

O RIGHTEOUS PERSON! I HEARD EVERY WORD YOU UTTERED: I RESPECT YOU FOR SUCH HONOURABLE SENTIMENTS!

PLEASE COME TO MY COURT AND BE MY CHIEF MINISTER.

I THANK YOU FOR YOUR OFFER, O MIGHTY KING, BUT...

...I DO NOT WANT LUXURY SUCH AS COURT LIFE AFFORDS. I HAVE NEVER SERVED ANOTHER. I AM QUITE HAPPY WHERE I AM.

HOWEVER, IF YOU STILL WISH TO APPOINT ME, I WILL OBEY — PROVIDED YOU TREAT MY ADVICE WITH RESPECT AND ALLOW ME TO GIVE IT TO YOU IN PRIVATE.

I GLADLY AGREE TO YOUR CONDITIONS!

SO THE JACKAL WENT TO THE COURT AND WAS TREATED BY THE KING WITH GREAT RESPECT.

OH! SO THAT'S THE NEW CHIEF MINISTER.

OH! HE'S JUST ANOTHER JACKAL! IF WE CONFIDE IN HIM, HE'LL SOON DO US OUT OF EVERYTHING WE HAVE!

THEY SAY HE IS HONEST. SHOULD WE TALK TO HIM OF OUR TROUBLES?

BUT, GRADUALLY, THEY LEARNT TO TRUST HIM. ONE BY ONE, THEY CAME TO HIM WITH THEIR PROBLEMS.

MY SON WAS PUNISHED FOR STEALING. BUT HE WAS INNOCENT!

THEN WHO WAS THE REAL THIEF?

IT WAS ONE OF THE MAGISTRATE'S FRIENDS!

MY CHILDREN ARE STARVING AND WE HAVE NO FOOD STORED FOR THE RAINY SEASON!

HOW IS THAT? I KNOW YOUR HUSBAND WORKS HARD.

HE DOES NOT ALWAYS GET WORK BECAUSE THE JACKAL IN CHARGE WANTS A BRIBE FROM HIM!

THE JACKAL SOON SAW TO IT THAT THEY GOT JUSTICE. BUT THOSE WHO WERE EXPLOITING THE POOR ANIMALS WERE VERY ANGRY.

THAT MINISTER IS ONE OF US. WHY SHOULD HE SIDE WITH THE COMMON PEOPLE?

HE HAS DONE AN UNFORGIVABLE THING. HE HAS SET THE HARE FREE AND SENT OUR GOOD FRIEND, THE MAGISTRATE, TO JAIL!

IT WON'T DO! WE MUST GET RID OF HIM!

THEY LOOKED ABOUT FOR WAYS OF DISCREDITING HIM. ONE DAY —

LOOK AT THAT FRESH PIECE OF MEAT LAID OUT FOR THE KING!

TAKE IT AWAY AT ONCE AND PUT IT IN THE CHIEF MINISTER'S ROOM! LEAVE THE REST TO ME!

OH, THEY INTEND TO HARM HIM!

THE CHIEF MINISTER HAS ALWAYS BEFRIENDED ME. BUT HOW CAN I HELP HIM? I AM AFRAID THEY WILL HARM ME, TOO, IF I OBJECT!

MINUTES LATER, THE KING CAME IN.

WHO HAS DARED TO TOUCH MY PLATE BEFORE I HAVE EATEN?

SPEAK UP!

IT WAS NOT ONE OF US, YOUR HIGHNESS.

NO, NO, CERTAINLY NOT!

WE WOULDN'T DREAM OF DOING SUCH A THING!

THEN WHO WAS IT?

ER... ER... ER...

GR... RR... RRR... DON'T STAMMER! WHO DID IT? ANSWER ME AT ONCE!

IT WAS THE CHIEF MINISTER. WE SAW HIM TAKE THE MEAT AWAY TO HIS ROOMS.

IT CAN'T BE TRUE!

IF YOU WILL COME WITH US, YOUR MAJESTY, WE WILL SHOW YOU WHERE IT IS!

I DON'T BELIEVE THIS, BUT, SINCE YOU SAY YOU HAVE THE EVIDENCE, I'LL GO WITH YOU AND SEE IT FOR MYSELF!

THERE, IN THE CHIEF MINISTER'S ROOM, WAS THE MEAT, PLACED BY THE RASCALLY JACKALS!

SO IT IS TRUE!

HOW CAN I TRUST ANY- ONE EVER AGAIN? I THOUGHT HE WAS HONEST BUT THE FACT IS, HE IS ONLY ANOTHER JACKAL!

YOU TRUSTED HIM TOO MUCH, O KING! WE DARED NOT TELL YOU THE TRUTH ABOUT HIM BEFORE!

I CAN'T BEAR TO BE MADE A FOOL OF LIKE THIS! THE CHIEF MINISTER SHALL BE EXECUTED AT ONCE!

ASK MY GUARDS TO ARREST HIM!

SO THE JACKAL WHO WAS CHIEF MINISTER WAS PLACED UNDER ARREST.

SOON AFTER, THE KING'S MOTHER HEARD ABOUT IT AND HURRIED TO SPEAK TO HER SON.

THIS CANNOT BE TRUE! I AM CERTAIN THE CHIEF MINISTER IS INNOCENT, THE VICTIM OF SOME EVIL PLOT!

BUT, MOTHER, THE MEAT WAS IN HIS ROOM. I SAW IT WITH MY OWN EYES!

WHILE THEY WERE HOTLY DISCUSSING THE CASE, A JACKAL CAME IN.

O, KING, MAY I BE ALLOWED TO SPEAK? IT IS IMPORTANT!

THE CHIEF MINISTER IS INNOCENT! TO PLOT HIS DOWNFALL, MY FRIENDS LIED ABOUT HIM TO YOU!

YOU SEE! I TOLD YOU SO!

BUT WHY DID YOU NOT SPEAK UP BEFORE? WERE YOU NOT AMONG THE VILE JACKALS WHEN THEY TALKED TO ME A LITTLE WHILE AGO?

I REMAINED SILENT TO SAVE MY SKIN, FOR I WAS AFRAID OF THEM. BUT I PLEAD FOR YOUR GRACIOUS MERCY.

ALL RIGHT, YOU MAY GO THOUGH YOU HAVE BEHAVED LIKE A COWARD!

THE KING THEN SENT FOR THE CHIEF MINISTER.

GOOD JACKAL, I WAS WRONG TO MAKE SO HASTY A JUDGEMENT AGAINST YOU. PLEASE RESUME YOUR DUTIES.

O KING, FIRST YOU BESTOWED UPON ME THE HIGHEST HONOURS OF THE LAND. THEN YOU TREATED ME AS YOUR ENEMY.

I HAVE WRONGED YOU. I SHOULD HAVE JUDGED BY YOUR ACTIONS WHICH HAVE ALWAYS BEEN JUST.

TRUST ONCE LOST CANNOT BE REGAINED. SUCH A SCAR PERMANENTLY MARS RELATIONSHIPS. PLEASE GIVE ME YOUR PERMISSION TO GO AWAY.

HE THEN WENT AWAY AND SPENT THE REST OF HIS DAYS IN SOLITUDE IN THE FOREST.

THE SAGE AND THE DOG

IN A DENSE FOREST, INHABITED ONLY BY WILD ANIMALS, THERE ONCE LIVED A GOOD RISHI. THE WILD CREATURES LOVED HIM AND CAME TO HIM TO BE TAUGHT BY HIM.

THAT DOG IS THE MOST DEVOTED OF ALL HIS DISCIPLES!

NEVER ONCE HAS HE LEFT THE SIDE OF HIS GURU!

AND WOULD YOU BELIEVE IT? THE DOG LIVES ON NOTHING BUT FRUITS, ROOTS AND WATER!

HOW EXTRAORDINARY! ARE YOU SURE?

I AM CERTAIN! LOOK AT HIM! HE'S SO WEAK AND THIN DUE TO FASTING.

ONE DAY, IT SO HAPPENED THAT A LEOPARD STRAYED INTO THE HERMITAGE.

HUNGRY AND THIRSTY, AND HIS JAWS WIDE OPEN, THE LEOPARD LOOKED LIKE A SECOND YAMA.* AND HE WANTED TO POUNCE UPON THE DOG.

TREMBLING WITH FEAR, THE DOG TURNED TO HIS GURU.

OH HOLY ONE! THIS LEOPARD WISHES TO EAT ME! PLEASE... FIND SOME WAY OF SAVING ME!

DON'T BE AFRAID, MY SON! LET THY NATURAL FORM DISAPPEAR AND...

...BE THOU A LEOPARD!

* THE LORD OF DEATH

THERE WAS A BLINDING FLASH LIKE A SUN EXPLODING. THE DOG WAS TRANSFORMED INTO A LEOPARD WITH A COAT WHICH GLEAMED LIKE BURNISHED GOLD!

SEEING THIS MAGNIFICENT ANIMAL OF HIS OWN SPECIES, THE LEOPARD WHO HAD COME TO EAT HIM FLED.

SOME TIME LATER, A FIERCE TIGER CAME TO THE HERMITAGE.

GR...RR...

THE LEOPARD WHO WAS REALLY A DOG, CROUCHED IN FEAR.

WITH HIS INNER VISION, THE RISHI SENSED THE DANGER AND QUICKLY TRANSFORMED HIM INTO A POWERFUL TIGER.

SEEING THIS NEW TIGER, THE HUNGRY TIGER LEFT AT ONCE.

THE DOG, NOW TRANSFORMED INTO A REGAL TIGER, GAVE UP HIS FORMER AUSTERE DIET AND BEGAN TO SUBSIST ON OTHER ANIMALS.

ONE DAY, HAVING HAD A LARGE MEAL, HE WAS SLEEPING IN THE YARD OF THE HERMITAGE...

...WHEN A ROGUE ELEPHANT CAME THERE, LOOKING LIKE A GREY CLOUD ON A STORMY HORIZON.

AS THIS ELEPHANT OF TERRIFYING PROPORTIONS APPROACHED, THE TIGER WHO WAS FORMERLY A DOG RUSHED TO THE RISHI FOR PROTECTION.

IN AN INSTANT, THE RISHI TRANSFORMED HIM INTO A MAGNIFICENT ELEPHANT!

I MUST BE GOING MAD! I THOUGHT I WAS CHASING A TIGER BUT HE APPEARS TO BE ONE OF MY OWN SPECIES!

HA! HA! HE'S GONE!

DELIGHTED WITH HIS NEW FORM, THE RISHI'S ELEPHANT WANDERED OFF TO A NEARBY LAKE, ENJOYING THE COOL WATER.

THEN ONE DAY, A SLAYER OF ALL ANIMALS CAME TO THE SPOT. IT WAS A SHARABHA, A TERRIBLE ANIMAL WITH EIGHT LEGS AND HE MADE STRAIGHT FOR THE RISHI'S ELEPHANT!

BUT THE ELEPHANT, THROUGH THE RISHI'S GRACE, HAD BECOME A SHARABHA, TOO. ONLY HE WAS BIGGER AND MORE FIERCE THAN THE OTHER ONE!

FRIGHTENED, THE SHARABHA BEGAN TO SLINK AWAY.

NOW OUR SHARABHA POSSESSED THE FIELD. BUT, WITH THE SUCCESSIVE CHANGES, HE HAD CHANGED IN OTHER WAYS TOO. NO LONGER DID HE LIVE ON FRUITS AND ROOTS. HE WAS NOW CONFIRMED IN THE HABITS OF A CARNIVOROUS BEAST.

23

AND NOW, EVER THIRSTING FOR FRESH BLOOD, HE WISHED TO SLAY THE SAGE!

THE SAGE DIVINED HIS INTENTION AT ONCE.

YOU DOG! IT WAS TO ME YOU OWED YOUR TRANSFORMATIONS AS LEOPARD, TIGER, ELEPHANT! AND FINALLY, HAVING BECOME A SHARABHA, YOU WISH TO DO ME INJURY!

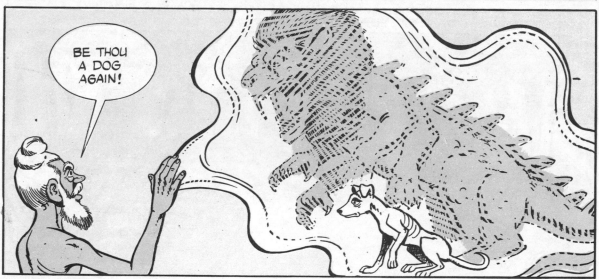

BE THOU A DOG AGAIN!

AS BEFORE, THE DOG RESTED AT THE FEET OF HIS GURU...

...BUT HE HAD BECOME VERY CHEERLESS. SO THE RISHI DROVE HIM AWAY.

GO AWAY, SINFUL CREATURE! NO ONE SHOULD BE PLACED IN A POSITION FOR WHICH HE IS NOT SUITED! YOU ARE CERTAINLY FIT ONLY TO BE A DOG!

THE SWAN AND THE CROW

THERE ONCE LIVED A CROW WHO WAS THE FAVOURITE OF THREE BOYS. EVERY DAY THEY FED HIM WITH THE REMNANTS OF THEIR FOOD.

COME, LOVELY CROW, WE WON'T HARM YOU!

EAT! EAT!

DOESN'T HE LOOK LOVELY?

LOOK AT HIS GLOSSY WINGS!

THE ADMIRATION OF THE CHILDREN FILLED THE CROW WITH PRIDE···

···AND HE BELIEVED HIMSELF TO BE THE HANDSOMEST, CLEVEREST BIRD IN THE LAND.

JUST THEN HE SPOTTED A FLOCK OF SWANS...

...AND THE SIGHT IRRITATED HIM!

STRANGERS HERE! THIS BEACH IS MINE, I WON'T TOLERATE ANY UGLY BIRDS IN MY TERRITORY!

THE LEADER OF THESE SWANS HEARD THIS AS HE WAS GLIDING BY.

UGLY, MY DEAR SIR! UGLY! HOW CAN YOU SAY SUCH A THING! NOBODY WOULD POSSIBLY DISPUTE A SWAN'S BEAUTY!

BESIDES WE ARE THE WORLD'S BEST FLIERS!

WHAT NONSENSE! ALL YOU CAN DO IS FLUTTER IN THE BREEZE LIKE A TORN RIBBON...

··· WHEREAS I ···! LOOK! JUST SEE WHAT I CAN DO AS A FLIER!

HE TURNED SEVERAL TIMES IN THE AIR LIKE AN ACROBAT.

HE MADE ZIG-ZAG PATTERNS IN THE AIR AND ···

···EVEN FLEW UPSIDE DOWN FOR A BIT.

GOOD LORD, WHAT A CLUMSY FOOL!

THE COMPETITION BEGAN AT ONCE.

THE SWAN GRADUALLY GAINED HEIGHT AND SPEED.

SOON HE WAS FLYING EFFORTLESSLY ACROSS THE OCEAN.

BUT THE CROW WAS SO EXHAUSTED HE COULD BARELY KEEP HIMSELF ABOVE THE WATER.

WHAT SHALL I DO? THERE IS NOT A TREE IN SIGHT! WHERE CAN I STOP TO REST?

HELP! OR I'LL DROWN!

JUST THEN THE SWAN RETURNED.

WHAT KIND OF FLYING IS THAT, FRIEND?

YOUR BEAK AND WINGS SEEM TO BE CONSTANTLY TOUCHING THE WATER!

OH, DON'T TAUNT ME! I AM SO TIRED! IN A LITTLE WHILE I WILL DROWN AND DIE!

TAKING PITY ON HIM, THE SWAN THEN TOOK HIM ON HIS BACK...

...AND FLEW TOWARDS THE SHORE.

HE PLACED THE CROW GENTLY ON THE SAND.

BROTHER SWAN! YOU ARE MY SUPERIOR! PROSPERITY MAKES FOOLISH ONES MORE FOOLISH. I AM INDEED ONLY A CROW. THANK YOU FOR PUTTING ME IN MY PLACE!

THE ANIMATED SERIES

The World of
Amar Chitra Katha
just got **More Exciting!**

The Tales of Arjuna

Abhimanyu

Also available:

Tales of Shivaji
Birbal The Wise
Hanuman To The Rescue
The Pandavas In Hiding

DVD Rs. 145/-

Mahiravan

Exclusive Games & Stickers Inside

To order: Log on to www.amarchitrakatha.com or
Call Toll free on 1800-233-9125 or SMS 'ACK BUY' to '575758'

Kumbhakarn